There was an old lady who swallowed a fly

illustrated by Pam Adams

Child's Play (International) Ltd
Ashworth Rd, Bridgemead, Swindon, SN5 7YD UK
Swindon   Auburn ME   Sydney
© 1973 M. Twinn   Printed in Heshan, China
ISBN 978-0-85953-018-7   HH180315NBH05150187
This impression 2015/2
www.childs-play.com

There was
an old lady
who swallowed a fly.
I don't know why she swallowed a fly.
Perhaps she'll die.

There was an old lady who swallowe
That wriggled and wriggled and jigg
She swallowed the spider to catch th
I don't know why she swallowed a fl
Perhaps she'll die.

She swal

catch the fly.

There was an old lady who swallowed a bird.
How absurd, to swallow a bird!
She swallowed the bird to catch the spider.

She swallowed the bird to catch the spider that wriggled and jiggled and wriggled inside her.

There was an old lady who swallowed a cat.
Well, fancy that, she swallowed a cat!
She swallowed the cat to catch the bird.

She swallowed the cat to catch the bird. How absurd to swallow a bird.

There was an **old** lady who swallowed a dog.
What a hog, to **swallow** a dog!
She swallowed the dog to catch the cat.

She swallowed the dog to cat...

...swallow a cat.

There was an old lady who swallowed a cow.
I don't know how she swallowed a cow!
She swallowed the cow to catch the dog.

She swallowed the cow to catch the dog. What a hog to swallow a dog.

There was an old lady who swallowed a horse.

There was an old lady who swallowed a fly.
I don't know why she swallowed a fly.
Perhaps she'll die.

There was an old lady who swallowed a spider,
That wriggled and wriggled and jiggled inside her.
  She swallowed the spider to catch the fly.
  I don't know why she swallowed a fly.
  Perhaps she'll die.

There was an old lady who swallowed a bird.
How absurd, to swallow a bird!
  She swallowed the bird to catch the spider. etc.

There was an old lady who swallowed a cat.
Well, fancy that, she swallowed a cat!
  She swallowed the cat to catch the bird. etc.

There was an old lady who swallowed a dog.
What a hog, to swallow a dog!
  She swallowed the dog to catch the cat. etc.

There was an old lady who swallowed a cow.
I don't know how she swallowed a cow!
  She swallowed the cow to catch the dog.
  She swallowed the dog to catch the cat.
  She swallowed the cat to catch the bird.
  She swallowed the bird to catch the spider,
  That wriggled and wriggled and jiggled inside her.
  She swallowed the spider to catch the fly.
  I don't know why she swallowed a fly.
  Perhaps she'll die.

There was an old lady who swallowed a horse.
She's dead of course.